In the Hush of the Evening

by Nancy Price Graff

illustrations by G. Brian Karas

HarperCollinsPublishers

In the hush of the evening
in the last of the light
at the close of the day
into the night
the whippoorwill sings
his song.
"Whip-poor-will," he calls
from the old pine tree,
"whip-poor-will."

At the top of the house
where shadows are deep
past the leaves of the trees
where the squirrels are asleep
a little boy waits and listens.
"Purr, purr,"
snores the tiger cat
curled on his lap,
"purr, purr."

Up the long stairway
from the lamplight below
through the damp stillness
in the deepening dusk
his mother comes
to kiss him good-night.
"Shh, shh," he whispers
in the hush of the room,
"shh, shh."

Together they sit
draped in a blanket
breathing in honeysuckle
hearing the night.
"Breep, breep,"
chirps a cricket
from the garden below,
"breep, breep."

Above in the ceiling
between creaky old boards
down from the attic
through channels well worn
a hungry mouse runs
on the prowl.
"Pip, pip," he squeaks,
nosing around
for a crumb,
"pip, pip."

Out of the gable at the peak of the roof
from a marble-sized hole into the yard
two furry bats swoop through the air.

"Swish, swish," whip their wings
close by the screen, "swish, swish."

At the rear of the barn
under the eave
to the left of the elm
near the crab apple tree
sounds the rattle
of garbage can lids.
"Just looking,"
the raccoon says
to her kits,
"just looking."

From the lip of the pond
where goldfish play
as dragonflies dream
at the end of day
the frogs' chorus swells.
"Good night,"
the giant bullfrogs sing,
"good night."

Out in the meadow
over sweet-smelling grass
above violets and daisies
under the stars
the fireflies dance.
"Blink, blink," they flash,
to the night music,
"blink, blink."

Beyond the meadow just past the woods
where the dirt road ends and pigeons roost
the church bell peals.

"Bong, bong," the big bell tolls in the night, "bong, bong."

Out in the forest
beyond the river
over the nests of swallows
sleeping, through the boughs
of willows leafing
comes the owl's question.
"Who's there?" he calls
in the pitch of the night,
"who's there?"

Up in his bedroom
close by the window
watching the moon
long after dark
the little boy
knows the answer.
"I am," he says
to the distant owl,
"I am."

Away from the window
now in his bed
snug with his lamb
bathed in moonlight
the little boy closes his eyes.
"Sweet dreams,"
says his mother
as she kisses him good-night,
"sweet dreams."

For my son, Garrett
—N.P.G.

For Carol and Patrick
—G.B.K.

IN THE HUSH OF THE EVENING
Text copyright © 1998 by Nancy Price Graff
Illustrations copyright © 1998 by G. Brian Karas
Printed in the U.S.A. All rights reserved.
Library of Congress catalog card number 97-34349
Typography by David Neuhaus and Elynn Cohen
1 2 3 4 5 6 7 8 9 10
❖
First Edition